HERA

Queen of the Gods, Goddess of Marriage

BY TERI TEMPLE

ILLUSTRATED BY ROBERT SQUIER

Published by The Child's World®
1980 Lookout Drive • Mankato, MN 56003-1705
800-599-READ • www.childsworld.com

Acknowledgments
The Child's World®: Mary Berendes, Publishing Director
The Design Lab: Design and production
Red Line Editorial: Editorial direction

Design elements: Maksym Dragunov/Dreamstime;
Dreamstime

Photographs ©: Shutterstock Images, 5, 15; Panos
Karapanagiotis/Shutterstock Images, 10; Africa
Studio/Shutterstock Images, 12; Mykhaylo Palinchak/
Shutterstock Images, 19; Igor Kovalchuk/Shutterstock
Images, 20

ISBN 9781614732617
LCCN 2012932423

Printed in the United States of America
Mankato, MN
December 2012
PA02157

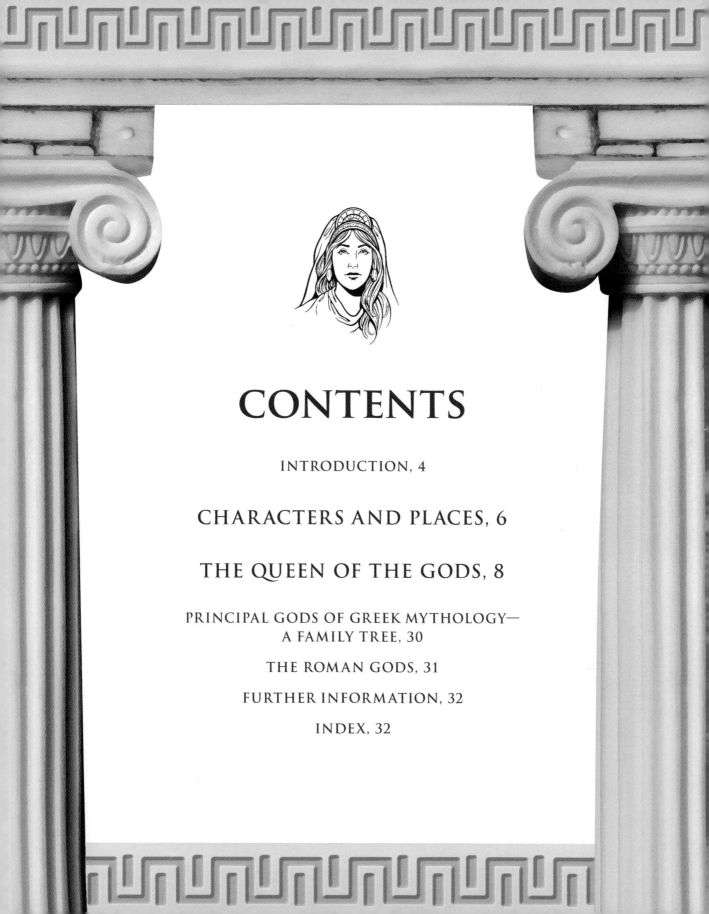

CONTENTS

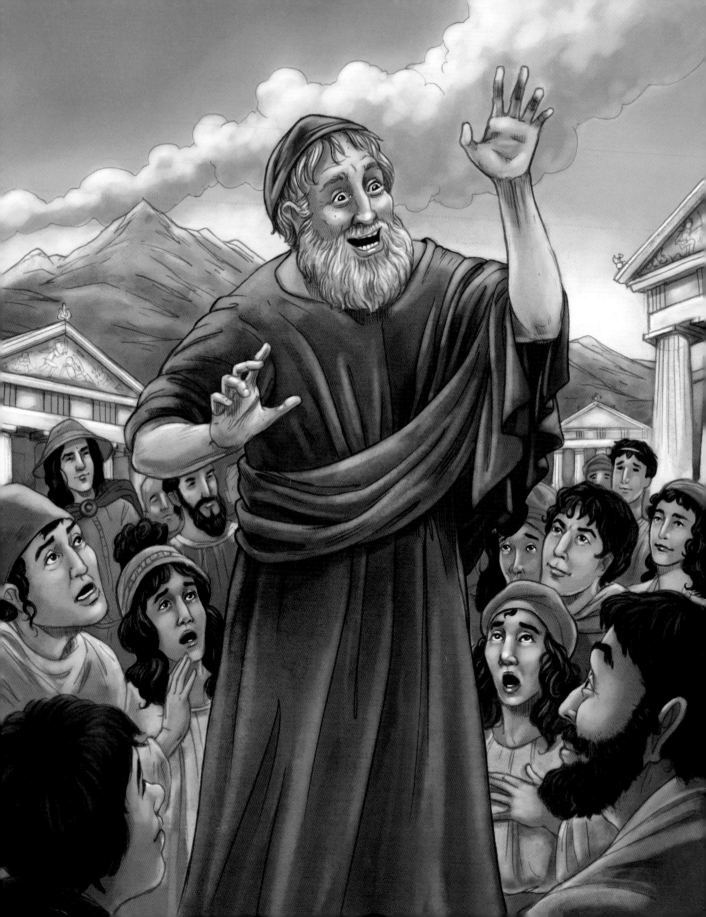

INTRODUCTION

Long ago in ancient Greece and Rome, most people believed that gods and goddesses ruled their world. Storytellers shared the adventures of these gods to help explain all the mysteries in life. The gods were immortal, meaning they lived forever. Their stories were full of love and tragedy, fearsome monsters, brave heroes, and struggles for power. The storytellers wove aspects of Greek customs and beliefs into the tales. Some stories told of the creation of the world and the origins of the gods. Others helped explain natural events such as earthquakes and storms. People believed the tales, which over time became myths.

The ancient Greeks and Romans worshiped the gods by building temples and statues in their honor. They felt the gods would protect and guide them. People passed down the myths through the generations by word of mouth. Later, famous poets such as Homer and Hesiod wrote them down. Today, these myths give us a unique look at what life was like in ancient Greece more than 2,000 years ago.

ANCIENT GREEK SOCIETIES

IN ANCIENT GREECE, CITIES, TOWNS, AND THEIR SURROUNDING FARMLANDS WERE CALLED CITY-STATES. THESE CITY-STATES EACH HAD THEIR OWN GOVERNMENTS. THEY MADE THEIR OWN LAWS. THE INDIVIDUAL CITY-STATES WERE VERY INDEPENDENT. THEY NEVER JOINED TO BECOME ONE WHOLE NATION. THEY DID, HOWEVER, SHARE A COMMON LANGUAGE, RELIGION, AND CULTURE.

MOUNT OLYMPUS
The mountaintop home of the 12 Olympic gods

Aegean Sea

ARGOS, GREECE
A city in Greece that was the center of worship to Hera

CRETE

ARGUS (AHR-guhs)
A monster with 100 eyes; Hera's servant

CRONUS (CROW-nus)
A Titan who ruled the world; married to Rhea and their children became the first six Olympic gods

CYCLOPES (SIGH-clopes)
One-eyed giants; children of Gaea and Uranus

ECHIDNA (ee-KID-nah)
Monstrous daughter of Mother Earth; mother to most of the monsters in Greek mythology

GAEA (JEE-uh)
Mother Earth and one of the first elements born to Chaos; mother of the Titans, Cyclopes, and Hecatoncheires

ANCIENT GREECE

**HECATONCHEIRES
(HEK-A-TON-KEAR-EEZ)**
*Monstrous creatures with
100 arms and 50 heads;
children of Gaea and Uranus*

HERA (HEER-uh)
*Queen of the gods;
married to Zeus*

**HERACLES
(HER-uh-KLEEZ)**
*Son of Zeus; hero of
Greek myths*

RHEA (RAY-uh)
*A Titaness; married to her
brother Cronus; mother to
the first six Olympic gods:
Zeus, Poseidon, Hades,
Demeter, Hestia, and Hera*

ZEUS (ZOOS)
*Supreme ruler of the heavens
and weather and of the gods
who lived on Mount Olympus;
youngest son of Cronus and
Rhea; married to Hera; father
of many gods and heroes*

Hera was the greatest of all the goddesses on Mount Olympus. Hera's parents were the giant Titans Cronus and Rhea. Cronus was the ruler of the universe. Shortly after his marriage to Rhea, Cronus learned of a prophecy. A prophecy is a prediction of what is to come. One of his children was destined to overthrow his rule. So Cronus swallowed his five children up whole. Hera was one of those children. It made Rhea angry and sad. When the time came to have her sixth child, she made a secret plan. She hid on the island of Crete. There she gave birth to her son Zeus. Cronus wanted Rhea to give him Zeus to swallow. But Rhea tricked Cronus. She gave him a stone wrapped in a blanket instead, which he swallowed instead of Zeus.

Zeus was allowed to grow up strong and healthy on the island. He planned to fulfill the prophecy. Zeus's wife Metis tricked Cronus into drinking a potion. This potion caused Cronus to vomit. All the children came out unharmed. They included the gods Poseidon and Hades and the goddesses Hestia, Demeter, and Hera.

Zeus led his brothers and sisters. Together they fought their father's forces for ten long years. Gaea, or Mother Earth, wanted the fighting to end. She helped Zeus. He was finally able to defeat Cronus. Zeus also had the help of the Cyclopes and their brothers, the Hecatoncheires. Zeus became the new ruler of the universe. His brothers and sisters would help him rule.

Peace settled over the lands. Zeus and his brothers decided to draw lots to decide where they would rule. To draw lots is to pick an object that represents a choice. When you pick, your decision is based on chance. Zeus drew the heavens. Poseidon drew the seas. And Hades drew the underworld. Hidden high atop a mountain in Greece, they built a beautiful palace. They called this place Mount Olympus. They would share Mount Olympus with all of the gods and goddesses. Together they would watch over the earth.

Hera was a beautiful goddess. It did not take long for Zeus to notice her. Zeus believed that she was the perfect match for him. She was powerful and bewitching. He wanted her for his wife. Zeus was used to getting what he wanted. So he was surprised when Hera did not quickly accept his offer of marriage. Hera was lovely, but jealous. She knew there were other women in Zeus's life. She did not want to share him with his other wives. So Zeus decided to trick Hera into becoming his wife.

MARRIAGE IN ANCIENT GREECE

IN ANCIENT GREECE, YOUNG WOMEN DID NOT CHOOSE THEIR HUSBANDS. THEIR FATHERS CHOSE HUSBANDS FOR THEM. IT WAS CALLED AN ARRANGED MARRIAGE. WOMEN DID NOT OFTEN OWN PROPERTY. SO THEIR FATHERS CHOSE MEN FROM THEIR OWN FAMILIES. THIS ALLOWED THE LANDS TO STAY IN THE FAMILY AFTER THE MARRIAGE. THE DAUGHTERS WERE OFTEN GIVEN A DOWRY. THIS WAS A GIFT OF LAND AND PROPERTY. IT WAS PASSED ON TO THE DAUGHTERS' SONS.

Zeus was the god of weather. He created a rainstorm. Then he disguised himself as a cuckoo bird. He sat on Hera's window and waited. She saw the shivering bird and took pity on it. She gathered the cuckoo up in her arms and brought it in to dry it off. Then the cuckoo turned into Zeus! Having won Hera's heart, they planned a wedding fit for the gods.

Nature itself celebrated their wedding. Flowers burst into full bloom. Zeus and Hera held a magnificent party at Mount Olympus. All the gods and goddesses attended. Even Zeus's brother Hades came up from the underworld. Mother Earth was so pleased she gave Hera a beautiful tree with golden apples. She planted it in the Garden of the Hesperides. A giant dragon with 100 heads was sent to protect the tree.

Zeus and Hera's honeymoon lasted for 300 years. For what is time to a god, when you live forever?

ANCIENT WEDDING TRADITIONS

THE WEDDING BETWEEN ZEUS AND HERA WAS USED AS A GUIDE FOR SACRED MARRIAGES IN ANCIENT GREECE. IT BECAME A TRADITION TO GIVE THE BRIDE GIFTS OF APPLES AND POMEGRANATES. THEY WERE HERA'S FAVORITE FRUITS. THE CEREMONY USUALLY BEGAN WITH THE WEDDING PARTY PARADING A STATUE OF HERA THROUGH TOWN.

Hera and Zeus ruled Mount Olympus as king and queen of the gods. Together they had four children. Their son Ares was the god of war. He was vain and had a bad temper. None of the gods were fond of him, not even his parents. Their daughter Hebe was the gentle goddess of youth. She was also a cupbearer to the gods and served ambrosia, the food of the gods. Their daughter Eileithyia was the goddess of childbirth. And the kind but ugly god of fire, Hephaestus, was their other son. Hera took one look at him and dropped him right out of Olympus. He fell for nine days. Hera claimed that he had no father. She said this because she was angry with Zeus over the birth of his daughter Athena. She was born from Zeus's forehead.

Life on Mount Olympus should have been perfect, but it was not. Hera was very jealous and kept a close eye on Zeus. Although he was the most powerful of gods, Zeus was afraid of Hera. He would often sneak behind her back to see his other wives. Zeus tried to stay out of Hera's way when she was in a rage. Hera's fits filled the palace. She made the other wives and children suffer.

THE TROJAN WAR

ONE EXAMPLE OF HERA'S GRUDGES WAS THE TROJAN WAR. THE WAR BETWEEN THE TROJANS AND THE GREEKS BEGAN AFTER A QUARREL BROKE OUT BETWEEN THE GODDESSES. A TROJAN NAMED PARIS JUDGED THE GODDESS OF LOVE, APHRODITE, TO BE LOVELIER THEN HERA. HERA WAS SO UPSET THAT HER RAGE LASTED UNTIL

Troy fell in ruins. A famous tale tells of how the Greeks tricked the Trojans. They entered the city inside a giant wooden horse given as a gift. At night, soldiers came out of the horse and attacked the Trojans. The war ended after that attack.

One poor maiden who suffered from Hera's rage was Io. Hera thought Zeus was on Earth to find a new bride. Zeus planned to meet Io. He made a thick cloud over the meeting place. Zeus thought it would cover his tracks. But Hera saw right through his plan. Just before she caught them, Zeus changed Io into a beautiful white cow. To protect Io, he claimed it was just an ordinary cow. Hera pretended to believe Zeus's story. She asked for the lovely cow as a gift. How could Zeus refuse his wife?

Hera took the cow and placed it in her garden. She tied the cow to an olive tree. Io was to be guarded by Argus. It was a monster with 100 eyes covering his body. He was Hera's faithful servant. Argus was the best watchman. He never closed more then half his eyes at a time. Poor Io was left to walk on four legs and eat grass.

Zeus could do nothing but watch Io suffer. He finally went to his son Hermes for help. Hermes was the cleverest of gods. He soon came up with a plan to help Io escape. He went down to visit Argus in the disguise of a shepherd. Argus was bored with only having a cow to watch day and night. First Hermes played him some music. Then he began to tell Argus a tale. It was a long and boring story that had no beginning or end. This made Argus sleepy. He closed 50 of his eyes. As the tale went on and on, Argus slowly closed the other 50 eyes. Hermes quickly touched all 100 eyes with his magic wand. It sent Argus to sleep and Hermes killed the monster.

Hera was fuming. Her favorite servant was dead and Io was free. Eventually, Hera let Zeus return Io to her human form. He promised to never set eyes on Io again. This was fine with Zeus. He had found a new love.

PEACOCKS

ANCIENT GREEKS BELIEVED THAT THE GODS CREATED NATURE. THIS IS THEIR VERSION OF HOW THE PEACOCK GOT EYES ON ITS TAIL. WHEN ARGUS DIED, HERA WANTED TO MAKE SURE HE WAS NEVER FORGOTTEN. TAKING HIS EYES, HERA PLACED THEM ON THE TAIL OF HER FAVORITE BIRD. ARGUS'S EYES WOULD NEVER SEE AGAIN, BUT THEY WERE BRIGHT AND BEAUTIFUL ON THE PEACOCK'S TAIL.

Callisto was a friend of the goddess Artemis. Zeus spied Callisto one day while she was out hunting. She was very beautiful. Zeus immediately fell in love with her. Hera soon discovered their affair. She learned that Callisto had given birth to Zeus's son. Hera wanted revenge. So Hera turned Callisto into a bear and left her to roam in the forest.

Hera was not finished. When Callisto's son Arcas grew up, Hera lured him into the woods. There she hoped he would shoot his own mother. Just as Arcas let his arrow fly, Zeus hurled Callisto into the heavens. Later Zeus transformed Arcas into a bear. He then set him in the stars near his mother to be her guard. Together their bear forms look down on us always. We know them today as the constellations, or groups of stars, of Ursa Major and Ursa Minor.

URSA MAJOR AND MINOR CONSTELLATIONS

IN THE NORTHERN SKY AT NIGHT, YOU CAN FIND THE CONSTELLATION URSA MAJOR (LATIN FOR "LARGER BEAR"). PEOPLE HAVE THOUGHT SINCE ANCIENT TIMES THAT THE STARS FORMED THE SHAPE OF A BEAR. SEVEN OF THE BRIGHTEST STARS IN THE CONSTELLATION MAKE UP THE MORE FAMILIAR BIG DIPPER. AND THE STARS OF THE CONSTELLATION URSA MINOR (LATIN FOR "SMALLER BEAR") MAKE UP THE LITTLE DIPPER.

Leto was another one of Zeus's unfortunate partners. Shortly after Zeus married Leto, they found out she was going to have twins. Hera flew into such a jealous rage that Zeus left Leto. Fearing Hera's wrath, no lands on Earth would offer Leto shelter. A giant serpent called Python chased her. But she finally came to the island of Delos. Poseidon had just created the island and it still floated on the ocean. Leto was able to give birth to her twins on the floating island.

The maiden Semele was not so lucky. After Zeus married Semele, he promised her anything she wanted. She just needed to keep their marriage a secret from Hera. But Hera learned of Zeus's betrayal and planned her revenge. She tricked Semele into asking Zeus to show his true form. Zeus knew no human could see him in his true form, but he had made a promise. When he showed himself as the mighty god, his thunderbolts killed Semele.

Hera's anger was not just directed at Zeus's other wives. She often punished Zeus's children as well. The child of Zeus who she hated most was Heracles, whose Roman name was Hercules. As a baby, Heracles was brought to Mount Olympus to live with the gods. Hera was not happy with this arrangement. She sent two snakes into Heracles's room to kill him. Heracles was not afraid and killed the snakes. The gods could see he would one day become someone special.

Heracles developed superior strength as he grew. He used this strength to rid the land of dangerous beasts. He became a hero. The King of Thebes offered his daughter to Heracles in marriage. Hera did not like this, so she drove Heracles to madness. He thought his wife and children were wild beasts and killed them all. Heracles was horrified by what he had done. He went to an oracle to find out what he must do to be forgiven. An oracle is a special priest who offers advice. The oracle told Heracles that he must complete ten tasks. Hera was elated! Heracles became the servant of King Eurystheus of Mycenae. Together Hera knew they could think of the hardest tasks for Heracles to perform.

Hera watched as the king sent him on his first four tasks. They included taking on two of Echidna's monstrous children. First he conquered the Nemean Lion. Then he fought the Hydra, a monster with nine heads. When it looked like he was close to killing it, Hera sent a giant crab in to cause problems. It did not stop Heracles. He was too strong and too clever. Hera and the king needed to come up with harder tasks.

Hera and the king sent Heracles to fetch the golden girdle of the queen of the Amazons. Surely the Amazons would stop him. Instead their queen fell in love with Heracles. Hera was so frustrated, she disguised herself as an Amazon woman. She spread a rumor that Heracles was there to kidnap their queen. The queen was killed in the battle that followed, but Heracles got her golden girdle. Two more tasks were added because Heracles had received help from the gods. But Heracles acted like a hero. He went on to live a full life. Upon his death, the gods, including Hera, welcomed him back to Mount Olympus.

Hera seems destined to be remembered only as the jealous wife of Zeus. Her bad temper and acts of revenge make Hera seem unworthy of worship by the ancient Greeks. Just the opposite was true. The ancient Greeks looked to Hera as the protector of marriage and women. The ancient people also prayed to her often during childbirth.

To the ancient Greeks, Hera was everything that was powerful and strong in women. They felt that she represented the three stages of life: childhood, adulthood, and old age. Hera was honored at many festivals as the goddess who cared for women. Following winter, the women in Greece would take Hera's statues to the river. There they would wash her statue as a form of rebirth. No matter how she is remembered, Hera played an important role in the ancient Greek myths.

HERA'S TEMPLE IN ARGOS

THE HERAEUM IS A TEMPLE DEDICATED TO HERA. IT WAS BUILT JUST OUTSIDE THE CITY OF ARGOS, GREECE. MANY TEMPLES WERE BUILT ON THE SITE OF THE FIRST ONE. THE MOST FAMOUS WAS BUILT IN 423 BC. IT WAS HOME TO A GOLD AND IVORY STATUE BY SCULPTOR POLYCLITUS THE ELDER. WHILE THE STATUE IS LONG GONE, COINS FROM THE TIME SHOW AN IMAGE OF THE STATUE'S HEAD.

PRINCIPAL GODS OF GREEK MYTHOLOGY –
A FAMILY TREE

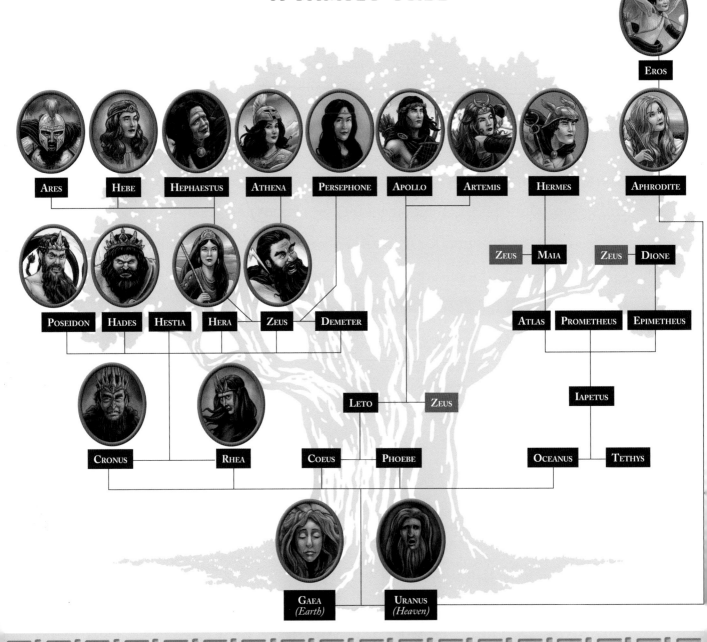

EROS

ARES · HEBE · HEPHAESTUS · ATHENA · PERSEPHONE · APOLLO · ARTEMIS · HERMES · APHRODITE

ZEUS · MAIA · ZEUS · DIONE

POSEIDON · HADES · HESTIA · HERA · ZEUS · DEMETER

ATLAS · PROMETHEUS · EPIMETHEUS

CRONUS · RHEA · LETO · ZEUS · IAPETUS

COEUS · PHOEBE · OCEANUS · TETHYS

GAEA
(Earth) · URANUS
(Heaven)

THE ROMAN GODS

As the Roman Empire expanded by conquering new lands the Romans often took on aspects of the customs and beliefs of the people they conquered. From the ancient Greeks they took their arts and sciences. They also adopted many of their gods and the myths that went with them into their religious beliefs. While the names were changed, the stories and legends found a new home.

ZEUS: *Jupiter*
King of the Gods, God of Sky and Storms
Symbols: *Eagle and Thunderbolt*

HERA: *Juno*
Queen of the Gods, Goddess of Marriage
Symbols: *Peacock, Cow, and Crow*

POSEIDON: *Neptune*
God of the Sea and Earthquakes
Symbols: *Trident, Horse, and Dolphin*

HADES: *Pluto*
God of the Underworld
Symbols: *Helmet, Metals, and Jewels*

ATHENA: *Minerva*
Goddess of Wisdom, War, and Crafts
Symbols: *Owl, Shield, and Olive Branch*

ARES: *Mars*
God of War
Symbols: *Vulture and Dog*

ARTEMIS: *Diana*
Goddess of Hunting and Protector of Animals
Symbols: *Stag and Moon*

APOLLO: *Apollo*
God of the Sun, Healing, Music, and Poetry
Symbols: *Laurel, Lyre, Bow, and Raven*

HEPHAESTUS: *Vulcan*
God of Fire, Metalwork, and Building
Symbols: *Fire, Hammer, and Donkey*

APHRODITE: *Venus*
Goddess of Love and Beauty
Symbols: *Dove, Sparrow, Swan, and Myrtle*

EROS: *Cupid*
God of Love
Symbols: *Quiver and Arrows*

HERMES: *Mercury*
God of Travels and Trade
Symbols: *Staff, Winged Sandals, and Helmet*

FURTHER INFORMATION

Books

Green, Jen. *Ancient Greek Myths*. New York: Gareth Stevens, 2010.

Napoli, Donna Jo. *Treasury of Greek Mythology: Classic Stories of Gods, Goddesses, Heroes & Monsters*. Washington, DC: National Geographic Society, 2011.

O'Connor, George. *Hera: The Goddess and Her Glory*. New York: First Second, 2011.

Web Sites

Visit our Web site for links about Hera:
childsworld.com/links

*Note to Parents, Teachers, and Librarians:
We routinely verify our Web links to make sure they are safe and active sites. So encourage your readers to check them out!*

INDEX